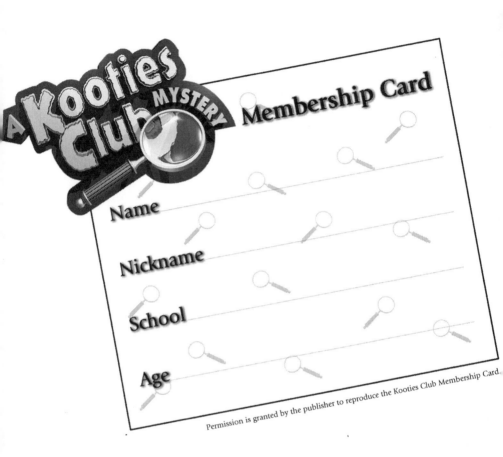

Membership Card

Name

Nickname

School

Age

Permission is granted by the publisher to reproduce the Kooties Club Membership Card.

The Mystery
of the Icky Icon

by M. J. Cosson

Perfection Learning®

Cover and Inside Illustrations: Michael A. Aspengren

For information, contact
Perfection Learning® Corporation,
1000 North Second Avenue, P.O. Box 500,
Logan, Iowa 51546-0500.
Tel: 1-800-831-4190
Fax: 1-712-644-2392
Paperback ISBN 0-7891-5253-3
Cover Craft® ISBN 0-7807-9668-3

5 6 PP 06

Table of Contents

Introduction

Abe, Ben, Gabe, Toby, and Ty live in a large city. There isn't much for kids to do. There isn't even a park close by.

Their neighborhood is made up of
apartment houses and trailer parks.
Gas stations and small shops stand
where the parks and grass used to be.
And there aren't many houses with
big yards.

Ty and Abe live in an apartment complex. Next door is a large vacant lot. It is full of brush, weeds, and trash. A path runs across the lot. On the other side is a trailer park. Ben and Toby live there.

Across the street from the trailer park is a big gray house. Gabe lives in the top apartment of the house.

The five boys have known one another since they started school. But they haven't always been friends.

The other kids say the boys have cooties. And the other kids won't touch them with a ten-foot pole. So Abe, Ben, Gabe, Toby, and Ty have formed their own club. They call it the Kooties Club.

Here's how to join. If no one else will have anything to do with you, you're in.

The boys call themselves the Koots for short. Ben's grandma calls his grandpa an *old coot*. And Ben thinks his grandpa is pretty cool. So if he's an old coot, Ben and his friends must be young koots.

The Koots play ball and hang out with one another. But most of all, they look for mysteries to solve.

Chapter 1

Computer Trouble

"Wow!" Abe stared at the computer. He could not believe his eyes.

Next to him Toby said, "Yuck, what's going on?"

Jade sat on the other side of Toby. She yelled, "Teacher!"

Mr. Freeman ran over.

"What's the . . ." Mr. Freeman stopped. He stared at the computer screens. He looked at Abe's screen.

Then he looked at Jade's. Then he glanced at Toby's.

"Move," he told all three kids at once. He sat down at Jade's computer. He messed with the mouse. He hit some keys. Then he said something under his breath.

Mr. Freeman turned off the computers.

He took off his glasses and wiped them on his shirt. He put them back on and continued to stare at the computers. At last, he turned to Abe, Jade, and Toby.

"Okay, tell me what that was all about," he said.

Abe looked at Jade. Jade looked at Toby. Toby looked at Abe. They all shook their heads.

"I just turned it on," Jade said.

11

"Me too," Abe said.

"Me too," Toby said. "I was going to do the math games. But that junk came on the screen."

Jade and Abe nodded.

Mr. Freeman took off his glasses. He wiped them on his shirt again.

"You had better go back to class," he said at last. He turned back to the computers.

Abe, Jade, and Toby left the computer lab. They walked down the hall. When they got to the door of their classroom, they heard a scream.

Abe pushed open the door. Ms. Morris was under the table. Her hair was in her face. She was tugging hard at a cord.

Ben sat at the computer. He looked surprised.

12

Thud! Ms. Morris landed on her
side. The plug was in her hand. It had
been stuck. When it popped out, she
had fallen over.

She sat up. She pushed her hair back from her face. Her eyes narrowed. She looked as if she might get mad.

"What was that?" she asked Ben.

"I don't know," Ben said. "All I did was turn it on."

"We had the same thing!" Abe, Jade, and Toby shouted. They told about the computers in Mr. Freeman's room.

Ms. Morris stood up. She brushed off her skirt.

"Well," she said. "I'll speak with Mr. Freeman. Now, class, it's time for silent reading. Take out your books."

Toby, Abe, and Ben looked at one another. They all had the same thought. This was a mystery for the Kooties Club.

14

Chapter 2

Koots on the Case

The Koots headed home from school. Ben, Toby, and Abe told Ty and Gabe about the computers.

"I smell a rat," Ty said.

"Where?" Abe stopped. He looked around.

"It means something is wrong," Gabe said. "Someone has done something bad. Acted like a rat."

"Oh," Abe said. "I get it."

"How are we going to figure this out?" Ty asked. "How could that thing get on all the computers?"

"Sounds like a network problem," Ben said. "Someone has gotten into the system. Probably a hacker."

"Hacker?" asked Abe. "Someone with an ax? What does that have to do with a computer?"

"Hackers are people who get into computers that aren't theirs. They can cause lots of trouble. They can even steal," Ben explained.

"That's probably what we have," Toby said. "A bad hacker."

"How can we trap this hacker?" asked Ty.

"I don't know," Ben said. "You would probably need to know a lot

16

about computers. We might be able to trace the hacker through the computer. He or she may have left a path."

"How do they leave a path?" Gabe asked.

"Not a real path. It's kind of like a trail that some computer people can follow," Ben said.

"All I know how to do is turn it on and play Math Facts," Toby said.

"Me too," Abe said.

"Me three," Gabe said.

"Me four," Ty said.

"I know a little more," Ben said.

"That's right," said Toby. "You're Ms. Morris's computer whiz."

Ben smiled. He was proud of himself. Then he frowned. "But not enough to track somebody down," he said.

17

Chapter 3

Geeks Wear Plaid

"I still think we can track down this hacker in our own way," whispered Gabe to Ty. They were hiding behind the bushes by Gabe's front porch. His big sister, Lisa, was on the porch. She was painting her toenails and talking to her friend Beth.

"I think you should go out with him," Lisa said.

"But he's such a geek," Beth replied.

Ty and Gabe looked at each other.

"A geek could be a hacker," Ty whispered. Gabe nodded.

"He's just smart," said Lisa. "There's nothing wrong with smart."

"He might be smart," said Beth. "But he's always in the computer lab. Only geeks hang out there. And he doesn't know how to dress. He wears plaid shirts. Nobody under 50 wears plaid shirts."

"My little brother does," said Lisa. "I guess he's a geek too."

Gabe frowned. "She knows we're here," he said. He stood up.

"Grandma gave me that shirt for my birthday. I only wear it around her," he said. He gave his sister a dirty look and walked away. Ty followed.

They went to Toby's. Ben and Abe were already there.

"Okay, Koots," Ty said. "How are we going to figure this out?"

"This is what I think we should do," Gabe said. "Somebody should talk to Mr. Freeman. Find out what he knows."

"Somebody should call that number Ms. Morris has by her desk. The computer hot line," Ben said. He looked around. The Koots stared back at him.

20

"Okay. I'll do it," Ben sighed.

"What else?" Gabe asked.

"There's a clue right on the computer!" Abe shouted.

"What?" Ty asked.

"That icky icon!" Abe answered. "It could mean something. It might be a clue!"

"Good going, Sherlock!" Gabe said. "Let's check these things out tomorrow after school."

Chapter 4

School Computers Are Down

Before school, the Koots split up.

"Can we talk to you?" Toby and Abe were standing in Mr. Freeman's doorway.

"Come on in, boys," Mr. Freeman said.

"You know what happened yesterday?" Toby began. "Just what did happen?"

Mr. Freeman took off his glasses. He rubbed the bridge of his nose. "Someone gave the system a virus. That icon has shown up on every computer screen in the schools. But it's worse than that. It ate up files. Teachers and students lost work. It was a very mean thing for someone to do."

"Can you trace it through the computer?" Toby asked.

"I don't think so. It did too much damage," Mr. Freeman said.

"We think a student did it on a school computer. It didn't hurt other computers. Just the ones that belong to the schools," Toby said.

Mr. Freeman shook his head again. His glasses were in his hands.

Abe and Toby headed for the door. "We're going to find that hacker for you," Toby said.

23

"Good luck, guys," Mr. Freeman said.

Meanwhile, Ben copied down the computer hot line 800 number. He would call it after school.

Abe sat at his desk. He shut his eyes. He tried to remember what the icky icon looked like. It had come on the screen so fast. Soon, it had filled the whole screen. He thought it looked like something had been blown up. He was sure he had seen it before. He just couldn't place it. He picked up his pencil. He started to doodle. His stomach growled.

Ty and Gabe decided to find the geek in the plaid shirt. After school, they would walk to the high school. They'd stand across the street and watch for the geek.

At the end of the day, each student was given a note from school. It read

Dear Families,
As you know, the Popco Company has given each school 20 computers. We are very thankful. We hope to put this gift to good use.

However, someone has tied up the system. We cannot use our new computers.

We need to find the person who did it.

If you know anything, please contact your school principal at once.

Thank you for your help.

Chapter 5

Koots Have a Plan

After supper, the Koots met at Ty's. "I called the 800 number," Ben said.

"What's the news?" Ty asked.

"They said they couldn't help me with the problem," Ben said. "I don't think they were too happy to talk to a kid."

"Heard that one before," Gabe said.

"We went looking for a high school geek," Ty said. He and Gabe laughed.

"Yeah," Gabe said. "We thought that there would only be one geek at the high school. But there's a whole bunch of them. Boys and girls. So now what do we do?"

"We could each pick one to talk to," Ben said. "Maybe we should all go to the high school tomorrow after school."

"Then what?" Ty asked.

"I don't know," Ben said. "Maybe we could each go up to one. And we could ask some questions. If somebody acts funny, that would be the one to zero in on."

Ben stopped. He was shy. It was a good idea. But would he have the nerve to do it? It had been a big deal for him to call the 800 number.

Toby looked at him. He knew what was going through Ben's head. Ben's face was getting red. He always got red when he got shy.

"You can talk to my brother, can't you?" he asked Ben.

Ben nodded.

"Well, he's almost in high school," Toby said. "What are these big kids going to do to us anyway? We'll go together. We'll pick them as they come out of the school. We won't go anywhere with them. We'll just ask them some questions right there. We'll all stick together."

"Sounds like a good idea to me," Gabe said.

Everybody nodded. Ben even moved his head up and down a little.

Abe had been quiet the whole time. At last, he spoke.

"I know I've seen that icon before," he said.

Ty looked at him. "What is it?"

"I don't know," said Abe. "It's hurting my head to think about it so much."

"Well, then give it a rest," said Toby. "Sometimes when you quit trying to think of something so hard, it just comes to you."

"Yeah," Abe said. He started wondering if his mom would pop some popcorn for him.

"Think I'll go home now," he said.

"Okay, let's meet after school by the front door. We'll walk to the high school together," Gabe said.

"Let's be thinking of good questions," Ben said.

The Koots wandered off to their own homes. Ben was the only one who thought about questions.

Chapter 6

Questions

The Koots walked to the high school. They stood outside as the big kids came out.

"They all look so big," Abe said.

"So what?" asked Ty. "We'll be that size in a few years. Take it easy. Big kids are just like us, only bigger."

"Yeah, right," Toby said. He rolled his eyes.

"Which ones are geeks?" Ben asked.

"The geeks come out last," Gabe said. "They are the ones who stay after school."

"Do you guys have questions ready?" Ben asked.

Toby looked at Ty. Ty looked at Abe. Abe looked at Gabe. They all looked at Ben.

"No," they said.

"I figured," Ben said. "This is what I came up with. We go up to the geeks and say we're writing for our school paper. We want to know what they think about the new computers."

"Sounds good," Abe said. "Except we don't have a school paper."

"We can say it's new. If they ask," Gabe said.

31

"After we say that, then we ask these questions," Ben went on.

"Shoot," said the rest of the Koots.

"One," said Ben. "Do you spend a lot of time on the computer?"

"Good one," Toby said.

Ben nodded. "Two," he said. "What's the hardest thing you know how to do on the computer?"

"That's good too," Gabe said.

"Three," said Ben. "What do you think happened to the school computers?"

"Then what?" asked all the Koots together.

"Then we watch their eyes. If they have a funny look, we dig deeper," Ben said.

"How do we dig deeper?" Ty asked.

"We'll need to get their names," Gabe said. "We can say we need it for the paper. Then we can learn more about them later."

"Right," Toby said.

"Look," Abe said. His eyes were on the door. It opened slowly. More students walked out. "Are they geeks?"

"Take a guess," Ty said. The students all had book bags. Some wore glasses. Two boys wore plaid shirts. There were a couple of girls too. They looked like ordinary teens.

"Let's go, troops," said Ty. He walked over to one of the teens. Each Koot chose a different one. They asked Ben's questions.

Five minutes later, the Koots were done.

"Did anybody get anything?" Ben asked.

"Nope," said Abe.

"Mine wasn't even a geek," said Gabe.

"Mine wouldn't talk to me," said Toby.

"I talked to two girls," said Ty. "They both think it's terrible about the computers. They're glad we 'little kids' care too."

Ben looked at everybody. "Mine had shifty eyes."

"Wow!" said the others. "Did you get his name?"

"Aaron something," answered Ben. "I didn't get his last name."

"I asked him the last question. He looked away. And he never looked me in the eye again. Do you know what he

34

said? He said he didn't think it was a big deal."

"Wow," said Gabe. "Not a big deal. He must be guilty. Let's find out more about him."

"I know him," Abe said. "He works at the Mideast Market. My mom goes there all the time."

"Is your mom going back soon?" Ben asked.

"Probably," Abe said.

"Let's go to your place," said Gabe.

35

Chapter 7

The Threat!

The Koots crowded into Abe's small kitchen. It was full of spicy smells. His mom was stirring a pot on the stove.

"Mom, when are you going to the Mideast Market?" Abe asked.

"I just went today, dear," said his mom.

Abe's face turned purple. He wished his mom wouldn't call him dear. At

least, she didn't have to call him that in front of the Koots.

"When will you go again?" asked Ben.

Abe's mom looked at the boys. "Do you boys need something?"

"I was just telling them about how neat the market is," said Abe. "They'd like to see it."

"They are having some good specials right now," said Abe's mom. "I could go again tomorrow. I could stock up on a few things. How about after school?"

"Sure," said the Koots. Then they went into Abe's room. Abe shut the door.

Ty looked at Abe. "Thank you for shutting the door, dear," he teased.

Abe got purple again.

"Knock it off," said Toby. "I've heard your mom call you 'baby.'"

Now Ty was purple too. He dropped the subject.

Ben asked, "Won't it look funny if we all go?"

"Yeah," said Gabe. "Maybe just one of us better go with Abe. Let's draw straws."

Abe got some toothpicks. He broke one off. He held them out to the Koots. Ben got the short one.

"Should Ben go?" asked Ty. "That kid will know him. You know, since Ben already talked to him."

"He saw us all," said Toby. "It won't matter."

The next day, Abe and Ben went with Abe's mom to the Mideast Market. It had the same spicy smells that Abe's

apartment had. Jars and cans filled the shelves. And big bags of rice were stacked on the floor.

Aaron was putting jars on a shelf. Ben and Abe walked up behind him. They didn't know what to do next. He didn't seem to see them.

"Ahem," said Ben.

"May I help you?" Aaron asked. He turned around.

"Oh, it's you again," he said to Ben. "What do you want?"

"We came with my mom," Abe said. "She shops here."

"Yes," Aaron said. "I've seen you here before. Did you want something?"

"I'd like to learn more about computers," Ben said.

Abe looked at him like he was from another planet.

Aaron smiled. "This is a food store."

Ben got red again. "I know. But yesterday, I got the feeling that you know lots about computers. I want to learn more. Can you help me?"

"Do you have a computer?" Aaron asked.

"Just at school," Ben said. "Do you have one?"

"Just at school," Aaron said. "Guess I can't help you." He turned back to his job.

"Well, you could just tell me some things. For when the computers at school get fixed," Ben said.

Abe stared at Ben. He didn't know Ben could be so pushy. He was proud of his friend.

"What do you want to know?" asked Aaron. He kept stacking jars.

"Well," Ben said. "How do you get into a system? How do you make changes in a computer?"

Abe's mouth dropped open. Ben had guts.

Aaron's eyes got narrow. Ben felt like Aaron was looking inside his brain. Then Aaron snapped, "You think I did it, don't you?"

"No," Ben said. He backed away. "I don't. I just want to know how it could happen."

"You ask too many questions," Aaron said. "You'd better be careful. You could get in trouble."

Abe was ready to run out of the store.

"What do you mean?" Ben asked.

"I mean some people get upset." A jar crashed to the floor.

41

"That jar could be you," Aaron said.

"Come on," said Abe. "Let's get out of here, Ben.

"We'll wait outside," Abe called to his mom. Abe pulled Ben through the door.

Chapter 8

Case Solved

When they got home, Toby, Ty, and Gabe were waiting by Abe's apartment. Abe told them what happened.

"Way to go, Ben," Gabe said.

"But we didn't get anywhere," Ben said.

"We can keep working on it. That's all we can do," Toby said. The others nodded.

The next day, there was a new clue.

Ty had to go to school early to make up some work. He walked along behind three high school boys.

". . . shut it down for good," Ty heard. What were they talking about? He got as close as he could.

"I wiped out the grades. I shut down the whole school system," the biggest boy bragged.

Ty couldn't believe his ears. He started walking faster.

Bump! The big boys had stopped. Ty ran right into them. They turned and looked at him.

Ty took off. He ran as fast as he could. Were they after him? His head was pounding. Was that blood beating in his brain or footsteps? He ran all the way to school. When he got there, he headed for Mr. Freeman's room.

Ty ran in. He shut the door behind him. He was out of breath.

"I know who did it! I just heard him tell his friends!"

"Calm down," Mr. Freeman said. "Who is it?"

"I don't know his name," Ty said. He told what he had heard.

"What did he look like?" asked Mr. Freeman. "What was he wearing?"

Ty told everything he could think of.

"Thanks, Ty. I'll call the high school."

Ty went on to his class. He was sure he had solved the mystery. He waited all day to hear something. He checked with Mr. Freeman at the end of the day. He didn't have any news yet.

After school, Ty told the Koots that the mystery might be solved.

Chapter 9

False Lead

That night, Abe had a dream. As clear as day, he saw the icky icon. The colors changed. The shape changed until it became the shape he knew.

Abe's eyes flew open. He had to tell somebody. He looked at the clock. It said 12:30. It was too late to call anybody. He'd just have to stay awake all night.

Maybe if I eat something, it will help me stay awake, he thought. His mom had made popcorn balls for his sister's Brownie meeting. Abe went to the kitchen. He grabbed a popcorn ball and took it back to bed.

The next thing he knew, it was morning. He looked at the alarm clock. Had he had a dream? It seemed like he'd wanted to remember something. But what?

Abe got up and got ready for school.

In the middle of the morning, Ty was called to Mr. Freeman's room.

"Did you find him?" he asked.

"Well, not really, Ty. You see, some of the high school kids saw you and your friends hanging around the school. You were asking about the computers," Mr. Freeman went on.

"It seems this boy was playing a trick on you. He didn't have anything to do with the computers."

"Are you sure?" asked Ty.

"They checked him out. He isn't the one," said Mr. Freeman. "Sorry, Ty."

"Yeah, I'm sorry too," said Ty. He walked back to class. Big kids could be such pains.

Chapter 10

Case
Solved—Again!

It was late Friday afternoon. Abe
was tired. He started to doze off. He
put his head on his desk. He closed his
eyes.

Pop! There it was!

Abe sat up. His eyes were wide
open. He hopped out of his seat. He
ran out of the room. Ms. Morris looked
out the door after him.

"Keep working, class," she said. Ben and Toby looked at each other. What was going on?

After school, the Koots waited for Abe. He didn't come out. At last, they walked home without him.

Friday night after supper, the Koots went to Abe's. His mom came to the door.

"Abe can't come out," she said. "He's not supposed to talk with anyone. He'll see you soon enough."

As they walked away, Ty said, "What is that all about?"

"He knows something," Toby said.

Saturday morning, Abe's mom said the same thing. It was the same Sunday morning.

Over the weekend, the Koots found out more about Aaron. Gabe's sister,

Lisa, knew him. He had stayed late that day because he was in the school play. He had the part of a gangster. He wasn't a geek or a hacker. He was an actor.

"I can't wait until I'm a big kid," Ty said. "I'll get to play tricks on younger kids then."

"I guess Abe is our only hope," Ben said.

Chapter 11

Abe Saves the Day

On Monday morning, Abe's dad drove him to school.

In class, he smiled at his friends. He acted like he was zipping his mouth shut.

"We know," Ty said. "If you were really our friend, you would have told us."

"It's a police matter," Abe said. "That's all I can say."

At 10:30, the whole school gathered in the lunchroom. Mr. Freeman spoke.

53

"Good morning, boys and girls," he began. "I'm happy to report that the hacker has been caught. I'm also glad to say that he is not a student."

Mr. Freeman paused. He removed his glasses and wiped them on his shirt. Then he continued. "The person responsible had been fired from Popco not long ago. He was very upset. He got into the computer system. He changed the Popco logo."

The Koots all looked at each other. Of course! That's what Abe had seen. The logo was a popping kernel of corn. On TV, it popped right at you. When you started the computer, it was supposed to do the same thing.

But the hacker had changed it to purple, red, and brown. Now it looked like exploding frog guts. But if you

54

changed the colors to white and yellow, it was just popcorn.

"That's not all," Mr. Freeman added. "The hacker also gave the computers a virus. He thought he was harming Popco. But he hurt the schools."

"There is some good news," he went on. "The computers were new. Not much had been stored on them yet. And the Popco people will fix them. We are very lucky."

Everyone clapped.

"One more thing," said Mr. Freeman. "Many students tried to solve this mystery. Thank you all.

"But one student was able to come up with the answer. Abe, please come here."

Abe walked to the front of the room. He held his shoulders back. His head was high.

"You were a big help in solving the case," Mr. Freeman said. "The Popco people are giving you a case of Popco popcorn. Enough to last for a year. And they are giving the school enough Popco popcorn for a whole school party."

Abe smiled and said, "Thank you."

But, somehow, popcorn didn't sound all that good to him anymore.